THE MAID'S GROOM
MAIL ORDER BRIDES OF FORT REGENT

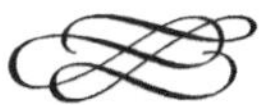

SUSANNAH CALLOWAY

Tica House
Publishing

Sweet Romance that Delights and Enchants!

PERSONAL WORD FROM THE AUTHOR

Dearest Readers,

Thank you so much for choosing one of my books. I am proud to be a part of the team of writers at Tica House Publishing who work joyfully to bring you stories of hope, faith, courage, and love. Your kind words and loving readership are deeply appreciated.

I would like to personally invite you to sign up for updates and to become part of our **Exclusive Reader Club**—it's completely Free to join! We'd love to welcome you!

Much love,

Susannah Calloway

VISIT HERE to Join our Reader's Club and to Receive Tica House Updates!

https://wesrom.subscribemenow.com/

CONTENTS

CHAPTER 1

Angela Rosewood ran her hand caressingly over the leather-bound books that filled the shelves, eyeing them like they were a horde of treasures. She wanted to know what the words said in those magical volumes. She knew she could be taken on enchanted journeys if she could just learn to read.

In truth, she could sign her name and read a few words, but she'd never gone to school. Her mother had died when she was six years old. Her father had kept Angie at home with just a neighbor lady to look in on her occasionally and drag her to church on Sunday along with her own brood of children. He worked at the boatyard during the day and spent most of the nights drinking. She learned to keep the house and cook a little, but she'd never learned to read. She'd never had the opportunity.

But she was learning now. Her heart pattered happily as she thought about the circumstances. She worked as a maid for the Donahues in their fancy house in Boston and somehow, she had caught the attention of their son, Marcus. When Marcus had found her in the library one day mooning over the books, it hadn't taken long for him to discover she didn't know how to read.

And now he was teaching her. She couldn't believe her luck. Every morning they slipped into the library because that was when she was scheduled to clean the room, anyway; it was his usual time for reading the paper. He had already taught her the alphabet and the sounds each letter made. She could make out simple words now and it was magical. She wanted to learn more and more. She wanted to learn not just to read but also to write.

And she wanted Marcus Donahue to fall in love with her; she knew that could never happen. She wasn't worthy of him—a servant girl and the son of the master? But a girl could dream.

Angie had plenty of dreams, big dreams. She dreamt of being an actress on the stage or a princess, or of traveling the world on a beautiful ship. The dreams were vivid and detailed, so detailed she could practically smell the sea air or feel the smoothness of the rich fabrics.

Sometimes, it seemed as if dreams were the only things that got her through the long, hard days she spent laboring at the

Donahues. She cleaned and swept and emptied chamber pots. It was her dreams that gave her pleasure.

Of course, sometimes the dreams got her in trouble, like yesterday when she was supposed to be sweeping and Mrs. Bagley, the housekeeper, caught her mooning at a painting of the coast, the ocean spreading endlessly beyond the sandy shores. Mrs. Bagley's loud 'harrumph' caught Angie by surprise, and she jerked so hard the broom she held knocked over a vase of flowers and sent roses and water flying everywhere, the vase crashing to the floor. To say the least, Mrs. Bagley was not pleased, and Angie's pay would be short this payday.

But she couldn't stop dreaming. She would just curl up and wither if she couldn't imagine a better life than she had now.

She plucked one of the books from the shelf and opened it, looking over the page carefully. She could recognize a few words but not very many. But it was better than a month ago when she wouldn't have been able to make out any of the printing.

"What are you doing there, Angie?" The voice came from behind her, and she jolted and the book flew out of her hand, landing on the floor with a dull plop.

"I'm sorry, Angie. I didn't mean to startle you." It was Marcus. Thank goodness—if Mrs. Bagley had caught her daydreaming again, she might have fired her. She lifted her gaze to meet Marcus's gray-blue eyes.

"Oh, Mr. Marcus, I should have known it was you. I just didn't expect you this early."

"I wanted to get here as early as possible. I wanted us to have plenty of time for your lesson."

She smiled gratefully. She couldn't tell Marcus how much this meant to her. He'd found a way to teach her to read, and she could still get her work done in a somewhat timely manner. He'd even been known to help her with the sweeping and dusting so she could spend more time working on her lessons.

"I brought you something," he said. "I thought you were ready for this."

He held out a book in his hand, and Angie gasped. "A book? For me?"

"For you. I'm afraid you'll find it a little childish but it has lots of simple words you'll be able to read, I think."

She took the book and held it tightly in her hands. "I've never had my own book before. Never a book of my very own."

"I hope this is just the first of many," he said, his gaze meeting hers. "You're going to love reading. I know you will. Go ahead, Angie. Open it. We'll read it together. Come sit on the settee with me."

She knew she shouldn't do it. What if she got caught sitting down with the master's son next to her? It would be a foolish thing to do.

But it was hard to resist the temptation. Not only because she wanted to delve into the book. Sitting next to Marcus was a tantalizing experience. She knew she would smell his special scent, the one that was like a tantalizing mixture of cedar and leather. If he sat close enough, she would be able to feel the heat from his body, too. The combination left her feeling all melty inside, and made her heart beat faster.

And she would be face to face with him. She would be so close she could see the dark, silky hair curling on his collar and the shadow of his long, thick eyelashes on his sun-bronzed skin. If he smiled, his dimples would be on display, and she would see the flash of his gleaming white teeth.

Ach, Angie knew it was dangerous, but she did it anyway. Her stomach turned somersaults when she took her seat on the leather, and Marcus sat down next to her. She couldn't help it. She sniffed, trying to catch a whiff of his elusive scent.

"All right, Angie, try to read the first page for me."

Angie focused and studied the print before hesitatingly beginning to read.

"The cat ran up the tree." Her voice sounded breathless to her own ears. She didn't know why she was so nervous.

Marcus had always been kind when she made a mistake. He was patient and didn't mind reminding her of certain tricks of the English language.

She continued on and read the short little story about a scaredy-cat afraid to climb down from the tree. The funny little book reminded her of a stray kitten she'd had when she was ten years old. She loved that kitty and let it keep her company often when her father was out. One day he'd come home and found the kitten in the house and slammed it against the wall. It never came back to visit again. She feared it had died, and she'd never forgiven her father for it.

Marcus looked over and smiled at Angie, his face growing soft. "You are progressing so well, Angie."

"Thank you, Mr. Marcus."

Suddenly, he reached over and tucked away a stray, coppery curl that had escaped the white cap she had to wear while she was working. The tip of his finger brushed her cheek as he pushed the curl back in place. Shocks ran through her body and a little gasp escaped her.

Their gazes locked as Marcus kept his hand where it was. Their faces were so close, Angie could feel his warm breath on her skin. Time seemed to stand still as she waited for his next move. *Oh my heavens,* she thought frantically, *I think he's going to kiss me.*

And he might have if there hadn't been a sudden rap on the door and Tilly, her friend and one of the other maids, came rushing in.

"Angie, Mrs. Bagley is looking for you, and she's on the warpath," Tilly squealed. "She'll fire you for sure if she finds you in here lollygagging with Master Marcus."

Angie jumped up, her heart racing. Marcus also jumped up.

"I'll go out through the solarium. Thank you for the warning, Tilly," Marcus said and turned and slipped out the French doors that led to the sunny solarium, his trim figure disappearing amongst the tall plants that inhabited the room.

Tilly stared at Angie, shaking her head hard enough that her cap slipped sideways. "Angie Rosewood, you are playing with fire."

Angie took a deep breath. If Tilly hadn't come in when she had, Marcus would have kissed her. She knew it.

"I-I know, Angie, but I can't stop myself. I-I am going to marry Marcus Donahue."

Tilly's mouth fell open, and she gasped. "Lawsy, Aggie, have you lost your mind? Even if Marcus wanted to marry you, his parents would never allow it."

Angie twisted her fingers in her apron. "I know, but it's something my gut is telling me. I will be Mrs. Marcus Donahue someday."

"You know you'll be fired if ya get caught mooning over him," Tilly said morosely. "You'll be out in the cold and then what?"

"I don't know," Angie said. "I'll have to trust in the Lord to help me if it ever comes to that. Now, I better go find Mrs. Bagley and see what she wants."

CHAPTER 2

Angie met with Marcus every morning for the next week. They worked on her reading and writing lessons regularly, but they talked, too, about all kinds of things. He loved to talk on a variety of subjects. Everything from items in the news, to places he'd been, to the newest advancements in industry, but he especially liked to talk about the wild west. It fascinated him and lured him like bait lures a fish.

One day he showed her a book, and they looked at pictures of places in the west. They gazed in wonder at snowcapped peaks and waterfalls that fell hundreds of feet. They saw buffalo and mountain lions, bears, and wild horses. Angie was almost as entranced by the pictures as Marcus was.

He pulled her over to a large globe and pointed at a spot on the map. "Look, that's Wyoming. Someday, Angie, I'm going to go there and see these mountains for myself," Marcus confided. "I don't know when, but I will go."

"But what about your family and your position with the bank?" she asked.

The thought of him leaving shot through Angie like an arrow piercing her heart, and her face took on a crestfallen expression.

"Banking is okay, but somedays it does seem a little boring. At least the surroundings are, stuffy old buildings and most of the customers are just as stuffy. Don't look so sad, I'm not going today."

Boring? Angie couldn't imagine Marcus ever being boring or bored. She thought he and his world were fascinating.

"I know, Mr. Marcus, but when the day comes, I will miss you terribly. You give me the only bright spot in my days."

They both stood with their heads bowed over the globe, each with a finger touching Wyoming on the map. He turned his head and looked at her, and a small smile playing across his lips.

"You are the sunshine in my life, too, Angie. Maybe someday we can go to Wyoming together."

Angie's heartbeat tripled its pace, and her green eyes grew wide. To go to Wyoming with Marcus was beyond what she could imagine, and in reality, she knew it would never happen. No matter how hard she wished it could be.

"Sure, and one day I'll be a princess and live in a castle," she whispered sadly. Depression overwhelmed her, and she turned and ran out of the room. She heard him call her name, but she didn't stop. She ran all the way to the broom closet and shut herself inside. She had to be alone for a minute.

Her breathing was shaky as she stood in the little room and let the tears come. She had to face reality. One day, Marcus would be gone. He would marry a rich socialite and would be out of bounds forever. The thought made her sick to her stomach, but she needed to accept the facts. Marrying Marcus Donahue was a fantasy, a dream that would never come true.

She whirled when the door was flung open, and she came face to face with Tilly.

"What on earth are ya doing in here, Angie?" the pixie-faced girl asked. "Hey, you're crying. What happened. Did that old bag Bagley catch you with Marcus?"

Angie sniffed and shook her head, unable to talk about it. "No, it's nothing, Tilly. I'm okay. I just got a little soap in my eye."

Tilly eyed her quizzically, a doubtful look on her face. "Okay, if you say so, but I'd be willing to bet this has something to do with Marcus Donahue."

"No, it doesn't, and if you tell anyone you found me in here crying, I'll never forgive you."

"All right." Tilly held her hands up defensively. "But I'm telling you, you'll quit mooning around over him if you know what's good for you."

Angie just nodded and shoved past Tilly, taking a dust mop with her. "I'll remember that. Now, I'm going to clean the foyer."

The next day, Angie didn't show up for her reading lesson. She decided she had to quit spending time alone with Marcus if she was going to get over him. There was no hope that they could ever be together. She was a maid, and he was a lofty member of Boston society. It would never work out.

Instead of cleaning the library that morning, she headed up to the ballroom. The Donahues were having a party Saturday night, and the room needed to be readied. Mrs. Bagley had asked her to see to it, and this morning was the perfect time.

She stood in the center of the spacious room and looked up. The glistening chandeliers towered above her, and she stared at them in awe. Just one of the chandeliers probably cost more money than she would make in a lifetime. They were perfectly symbolic of why she could never be with Marcus. In fact, this entire room was a tribute to his wealth and a reminder of her poverty.

The polished mahogany floors gleamed beneath her feet and gilded wallpaper covered the walls. Burgundy velvet drapes covered the many windows, and she ran a hand over the soft material. Even the drapes were of a finer fabric than she would ever own.

She glanced over at the raised dais where the orchestra sat during the Donahues' formal events. What would it be like to dance across these shining floors in a dress made of satin and lace? To listen to the beautiful music and float across the floorboards held in Marcus's arms?

Dreamily she lifted a pinch of her black skirt in her fingers and executed a dainty curtsey to her imaginary partner. She started to hum a tune she'd heard once and began to glide in smooth, graceful motions as she pretended to dance to music played by the orchestra. Oh, it was a lovely feeling indeed. Maybe it would never happen in real life, but she could enjoy imagining it could.

She whirled around still holding her skirt but froze when she saw Marcus standing before her, a dazzling smile playing across his lips. He approached her and bowed from the waist, his eyes twinkling merrily.

"May I have this dance, Miss Rosewood?" He held out his hand and took her fingers gently in his.

Angie's breath froze in her throat when his hand went to her waist, and he started to hum the same tune she'd been humming. He guided her through a few steps, and Angie felt as if she'd been transported to an enchanted place. Here, in his arms, it felt as if anything were possible.

And then it happened. He stopped dancing and lowered her lips to hers, capturing them ever so sweetly.

At first, Angie couldn't move, couldn't breathe. Then suddenly she gave in to the whirlwind of feelings washing over her. She drank in the taste of him like a woman dying of thirst guzzled the first water she'd had in days. She'd never before tasted anything so delicious.

He pulled her close, and her hands slipped around his neck. She rose on her tiptoes to get closer to him and let her fingers slide into his hair, the world swirling around her.

Then reality reared its ugly head.

She pulled back and pushed her hands against his chest. She turned away, unable to look at his dear face.

"Marcus, n-no. It hurts too much."

He turned her face toward him and ran his palm along her cheek, using his thumb to wipe away the single tear that rolled down her face.

"You know this will never work. I'm a maid and you're… well…you're rich. Society will never allow us to be together."

"Angela Rosewood," he said quietly, "my angel, I swear I will find a way. I will find a way to make this work, to make my parents understand that I love you. Trust me. Please."

Angie's gaze locked with his, and she drowned in those deep blue pools. Lord help her, she could be making the biggest mistake of her life.

But her heart said completely the opposite, and she nodded. She would trust him. She *did* trust him.

CHAPTER 3

Over the next few days, Angie was happy. Marcus *loved her*. He'd said so, and she believed him. She did her work as diligently as before, but she had a new curiosity about how things worked in this house. She wanted to learn it all. How to host a party, how to plan the meals, how to decorate the house. After all, if she was going to be Mrs. Marcus Donahue, she would need to know such things.

She spent as much time in the kitchen as she could, listening to Mrs. Donahue and Cook discuss the menus. Eavesdropping on Mrs. Bagley and Mrs. Donahue talking about the house became a habit. She lingered in the butler's pantry, watching the family and their guests as they ate, trying to learn all the etiquette she could.

Then one evening, Mrs. Bagley discovered her there peeking around the corner. The woman hauled Angie back to the kitchen and lit into her, calling her lazy and nosy, even accusing her of spying on the family.

"You will stay here and scrub the kitchen floors tonight, girl. Maybe some time on your knees will give you time to think about how lucky you are to have this job."

Angie wanted to tell the old biddy that she wasn't going to need this job for much longer, that she was going to be Mrs. Marcus Donahue, and then she could order this woman about.

But she managed to bite her tongue. She stood with her head bowed and her hands folded in front of her, simply nodding to Mrs. Bagley's orders. The older woman had never liked her. Angie didn't know why, but she'd recognized the venom in her eyes from the first day she'd started working here.

Later that night, when the other kitchen help had left for the evening, Angie was down on her hands and knees running a brush across the floor when Tilly walked in.

"Tilly, what are you doing here? You should be in bed."

"I came to help you. That way you'll get done that much faster. It's not like old bag Bagley will let you sleep extra in the morning."

Angie sat back on her calves and smiled at the freckle-faced girl. "Thank you. You are a good friend."

Tilly got another bucket and filled it with water. "What did you do this time to get her riled up?"

"I was hiding in the butler's pantry watching the family eat. I want to learn about etiquette and the way things are done."

"Why? Don't tell me you're still dreaming about marrying Master Marcus?" She put her palms over her face and shook her head. "You're going to get yourself fired."

Angie sighed and scrubbed harder. "Marcus loves me, Tilly. He told me so. He said he'll work it out so we can be together."

"And you believed him?" Tilly asked in an awestruck voice. "Don't you know that's the oldest line in the book? He'll tell you that right up until he gets you in a family way, and then he won't want nothing to do with you."

Angie's cheeks blazed. "Don't be silly. Marcus has always been a gentleman. We've only kissed. You can't get in a family way from kissing."

"Well, I'm just warning you. You've got to be careful or you're going to get fired. Especially if they think you're setting your cap for Master Marcus."

"Don't worry. Marcus asked me to trust him, and I do. Everything will be all right."

Those words echoed over and over again as Angie shoved her few personal belongings into a worn bag. She had trusted Marcus completely. She'd spent more time in the library with him, continuing her reading and writing lessons, but now there were stolen kisses included in their sessions.

She'd even snuck out and met him in the garden once or twice. They'd slipped into the gazebo and talked about endless topics, holding hands, and exchanging gentle kisses. She was always careful not to be seen.

Marcus brought her little gifts like books to read and ribbons for her hair. Her favorite was a pencil box with hearts engraved on it. When she'd opened it, she'd found it filled with pencils and there was even a pen and sealing wax and a stamp with an A on it.

Then two days ago, he told her he had to go to Baltimore on business and would be gone for at least three weeks.

"I don't want to go, but I have to. I promise, though, when I get back, I'm going to tell my parents about us. I can't wait anymore for us to be together."

He'd stroked her hair and kissed her goodbye. She thought she'd see him again in three weeks. Now she didn't know if she would ever see him again.

She clutched the pencil case to her and looked around the tiny room for anything she might have forgotten. That wasn't likely, she owned so little. All she had was a couple of dresses and a few bloomers and petticoats.

It was the worst day of her life next to the day her mother had died.

It had started well. The sun had been shining, and the temperature was mild. Cook was jovial that morning, and even gave Angie an extra biscuit with breakfast. That had seemed like a good omen.

Then Mrs. Bagley had come in with a scowl on her face and demanded Angie accompany her to the little room she used for an office.

"I know what you've been up to, young lady and you're not going to get away with it."

Angie's stomach lurched as she looked at the woman's angry face. What had she done now?

"I saw you trying to seduce Marcus. I saw you playing kissy-face with him in the garden. You left me no choice but to report your indiscretion to Master and Mistress Donahue. They have ordered me to terminate your employment at once. And in case you don't know what that big word means, it means you are fired." Agnes Bagley crossed her arms in front of her, a smug look on her face. "You are to pack your things and leave the premises immediately.

Angie's mouth opened and then snapped closed. What could she say? Marcus wasn't here to defend her, and there was nothing she could say that would make the Donahues change their mind. She'd whirled around and left the room.

Now she was packed and ready to leave, but where was she to go?

CHAPTER 4

One week later, Angie lay curled on a lumpy mattress with three little girls beside her. She tried to roll over but ended up with little Moira's foot in her face instead.

She sighed and closed her eyes, determined to get more sleep than she had the last few nights. When she'd left the Donahues', she'd been terrified, afraid that she would have to sleep on the streets. Fortunately, though, Tilly caught her as she was going out the back door and gave her the address of her sister. "Go there, tell her I sent you. Hazel and her husband will put you up for a few days."

So that was exactly what she'd done. She felt like she was begging, but at least it was a roof over her head, and Hazel fed her enough to survive.

It wasn't ideal, though, for sure. There were five children, Hazel, and her husband, Burt. It was crowded and humble. Angie slept in the bed with the three little girls while Tilly, who was presently staying there, too, took the couch.

Not only was space a problem, but Angie felt like she was taking food out of their mouths. There was little income and nine people to feed. Hazel worked magic with beans and potatoes, but Angie still felt guilty with every bite she took.

Her options were almost non-existent, but she knew she had to go somewhere. She'd been looking for a job all week with no luck. She didn't have any references, which all the prospective employers wanted. She couldn't stay here much longer, that was certain. If only Marcus were here, he would help, but he wasn't, and Tilly told her that his trip had been extended, and it would be at least four weeks before he would be back.

All she could do was pray that God would help her find her way. She reminded herself that things could be worse, but she wasn't sure exactly how. All she could see right now was a bleak future of hunger and homelessness.

With that thought, she cried herself to sleep as she prayed to God to give her a sign and some kind of direction.

The next morning, Angie hit the streets and started job hunting again. She had to go a little farther today because she'd already tried all the places closer to Hazel's.

By the time noon came, her feet were aching and her back hurt. She'd had no better luck finding work today. Her stomach growled, and she was thirsty, but she couldn't spare a penny for food or drink.

She was passing a small office when a flyer on the window caught her eye.

Be a Mail Order Bride. Travel West and get married. All expenses paid.

Angie stopped in her tracks and studied the poster, slowly making out the words. Could this be the sign she'd asked God for?

She hesitated. What exactly did it mean? She would have to marry a stranger and spend her life with him?

But she would have food and a roof over her head which is more than she would soon have. And she would get to travel to the west, the very place Marcus had dreamed of visiting. She had to admit, she had dreamed of it, too, but her dream involved going there with Marcus.

There was a rap on the window, and Angie looked up to see a pudgy-faced, gray-headed woman with a big smile on her face waving for her to come inside. Angie didn't know what to do, but curiosity finally won out, and she turned to go in the door.

"Hello. I'm Delia Rogers. I saw you looking at our advert and wanted to tell you more about the program."

Angie clutched her reticule close and let Mrs. Rogers lead her to a chair next to a desk. They both took a seat, and Mrs. Rogers started talking. She told Angie about the application and the many men who were anxiously waiting for brides in the west. She said the trip would be made by train and depending on where the bride's destination was, maybe a little bit of stagecoach travel would be involved as well.

"And best of all, you get to go to the West where everyone is starting new. The country is beautiful, and it won't cost you a dime. Now, the process normally takes a few weeks so would you like to get started?"

Angie's stomach fell when she heard that statement. She didn't have a few weeks.

She shook her said and said, "I'm sorry. I need someplace to go now. It was just a thought, anyway."

"You don't have any place to go, do you, dear?" Delia asked quietly. "Give me just a minute, won't you?"

She shuffled through some papers on the desk and pulled a letter out from the stack.

"You know, I may have the solution. This marriage was all arranged when suddenly, the bride backed out. Said she'd found someone to marry here. Her tickets were bought and everything. Yes, here it is. Mr. Robert Beekman of Fort Regent, Wyoming. He's a rancher out there and promises a good home would be provided. You'd have to leave tomorrow, though. That's when the tickets are for."

Angie twisted her reticule around her wrists much like her stomach twisted at the thought of taking this bold move. This was a life-changing decision. Yes, it would be a solution to the immediate problem, but how would it work out in the long run? What if she hated the man she was supposed to marry? What if she hated the West? She'd never lived anyplace but Boston. The pictures of the place were beautiful and provoking but living on the frontier was a far cry from living in Boston.

And, most of all, it would mean giving up her dream of marrying Marcus Donahue, the man she loved. She would never get to hold him or kiss him again, never hear the velvety timbre of his voice, never feel the touch of his hand on her cheek again.

Then reality slapped her in the face. She knew it was never going to happen. Marcus's parents would do everything in their power to stop their son from marrying a servant girl. If he defied them, they would cut him off without a dime. She couldn't do that to him.

Her heart sank as she raised her chin. "All right. I'll do it."

CHAPTER 5

Angie tried to calm her nerves as the train puffed along the tracks. It felt as if she'd been riding forever, rocking along through towns and countryside, past fields and forests, across rivers, and uphill and down. She wasn't sure they would ever arrive in Fort Regent.

She still couldn't believe she had done this. She was traveling clear across the country to marry a man she had never met, never laid her eyes upon. She was committing her life forever to a complete stranger. What if he was mean and nasty? What if he didn't bathe or shave? What if he was shiftless and didn't really have a house to take her home to? Worse yet, what if he was a wife-beater?

Tilly had told her she was crazy. "Are ya joshing me?" she'd squawked. "You'd have to crawl into bed with some strange man? That would be awful."

"I know, but what else am I supposed to do? My heart says don't do it, wait here for the slim possibility that Marcus will save me, but my head tells me this is my only real choice."

Fear churned in her stomach like an angry whirlpool. This was either going to be the best thing she had ever done…or the worst. It could go either way.

A voice broke into Angie's reverie.

"Here, dear, I get off at the next stop," a middle-aged woman with kind eyes said to her. "Why don't you take this extra sandwich and apple I have leftover?"

Angie looked up and smiled. "Thank you so much, but I'm just going to Fort Regent. Isn't that the stop after this one?"

"Yes, it is, but it's still a good hour or two away. Take them, won't you? You look pale. You must be hungry."

Angie blushed but finally accepted the offerings. She was hungry. The Mail Order Bride agency had given her a small stipend for traveling money, but it was almost gone.

"Thank you. I do appreciate it."

"You're welcome, dearie. And good luck wherever you are going."

The woman's kind smile was almost Angie's undoing. She had to fight off the urge to throw herself in the motherly woman's arms and sob out her whole story, but she managed to refrain herself and waved as the woman prepared to leave the train. Next stop, Fort Regent.

"Are you Angela Rosewood?"

Angie looked up into the meanest eyes she'd ever seen. They were the color of tarnished gold and guarded by thick, bushy, dark eyebrows. The orbs were small and set close together and had a gleam in them that sent shivers down Angie's spine.

She finally managed to squeak out an answer. "Y…yes, I'm Angie Rosewood."

"Well, I'm Robert Beekman, your future husband." He puffed up his brawny chest and pulled himself up to his full height, which must have been all of five feet six inches tall.

He was stocky and had shaggy black hair hanging below his cowboy hat. It looked like it hadn't been washed for a while. Dark stubble covered his cheeks, and Angie noticed a spot on his shirt that might have been from some slopped gravy.

Angie swallowed as she stared up at the leering face of her fiancé. Goodness, if this was how he looked when he came to first meet her, she hated to think what he must look like on a normal day at home.

"How do you do?" she managed to whisper.

"Just fine, little lady, just fine." He ran his gaze up and down her figure and tipped her chin up with his finger so he could study her face. "Say, that there marriage agency did okay for itself. You are a pretty little thing, ain't ya? Probably a lot better lookin' than that first wench they were gonna send."

Hot color flooded Angie's cheeks.

"Course, you're a might little to do all that work out on the ranch. Think you'll be able to handle doin' laundry and haulin' wood? Course, you'll need to cook and clean and help a bit with the livestock, too."

"I can handle it. I'm stronger than I look." Angie stuck her chin out stubbornly. How dare this man critique her on her looks before she even had a chance? He acted as if he were buying a horse. She almost offered to show him her teeth.

"Well, I sure hope so. I've got a lot of dough wrapped up in you already, and I still got to pay for your room and board until the preacher gets back in town and can hitch us. That will be about three weeks from now."

Angie didn't really know how to respond to that, so she just shrugged and said, "I think you'll get your money's worth."

"I hope you're right. I tend to get a little angry when people welch on a deal. Well, come on, I'll take you over to Mrs. Brady's where you'll be staying."

Angie clutched her faded, old carpetbag and noticed he didn't offer to carry it for her as he began to stride away from the depot. She had to hurry to keep up with the man, her bag banging into her calves as she almost ran to stay next to him.

"Is it far to Mrs. Brady's?" she asked when she was beside him again.

"Nah, it's just down the street. Ain't nothin' far in this little hick town." He walked another block past a general store and two saloons and turned up the walk of a white frame house. "This is it."

He walked across a broad porch and knocked on the door, leaning nonchalantly against the door frame as he waited. When it opened, he straightened and tipped his hat.

"Howdy, Mrs. Brady. I brought my bride. This here is Angela Rosewood."

"Well, hello and welcome. Won't you come in?"

Relief flooded through Angie at the sight of the friendly face. Warm blue eyes sparkled beneath a headful of nut-brown curls. Apple-cheeked and freckled, her face was a wreath of smiles, and she was a bundle of energy. She quickly took Angie's bag and hustled her into the sitting room. "My name's Maggie, and I'm glad you're here. Sit down, Angie. I'll get us something cold to drink and some cookies."

In a flash, Maggie was gone again, and Angie found herself alone with Robert Beekman.

"Well, I'm going to get back to the ranch, little missy, but I'll be back tomorrow to take you out and show you the place. Give ya a look at where you're going to spend the rest of your life." He chuckled, tipped his hat, and was gone.

Tears burned Angie's eyes as she watched his departing back. Dearest God, she didn't think she could go through with this.

She could not marry Robert Beekman.

CHAPTER 6

Angie spent the evening with Maggie, her two children, and her two male boarders. Maggie had thirteen-year-old twins, a boy, and a girl, named Kevin and Katie. The boarders were both older gentlemen, one a clerk in the general store, and Mr. Little who worked at the train station. They all enjoyed a pot roast dinner with chocolate cake for dessert. When the meal was finished, Angie insisted on helping to clean up. She wouldn't feel right sitting by and letting someone else do all the dishes.

Angie finished wiping off the table and sighed. She was tired. It had been a long, arduous train journey to get here. She prayed she hadn't made a mistake but feared she might have. Robert Beekman wasn't her dream mate, for sure.

"How about a nice cup of tea and a little girl talk before bed," Maggie said, reaching for the kettle. "Katie, you better go on to bed. You've got school in the morning."

"Oh, Mom, can't I stay up and talk to Angie, too?" Katie pleaded. "I'd love to hear more about Boston."

"Come talk to me tomorrow when you get home, Katie. I'll be happy to tell you all about it then if you'd like," Angie assured her.

Once Katie was gone, Angie sat down at the kitchen table and Maggie got the tea ready. Angie wrapped her hands around the cup and let the soothing heat comfort her.

"So, how did you meet Mr. Beekman?" Maggie asked as she took the seat opposite Angie.

Color rushed to Angie's cheeks as she made her confession. "Actually, I just met him today. I'm what they call a Mail Order Bride."

"You mean he *bought* you?" Maggie looked incredulous.

"I guess that's what it boils down to." Angie shrugged. "He paid for my trip here and will marry me and put a roof over my head for the rest of my life."

"I see. I guess I just can't imagine marrying like that. I knew my husband Tom most of my life. When he decided he wanted to come from St. Louis out here, we were already married."

"Are you glad you came?"

"Oh, yeah, I think so. It was a good life up until Tom died from pneumonia five years ago. He'd done well for himself. We had a good ranch that was doing well. After he died, I sold the ranch and bought this house. Ranch life is hard on a woman, especially when she doesn't have a man around."

Angie nodded. She could see how running a ranch and raising two young children would be difficult. "Mr. Beekman, er Robert, is taking me to see his home tomorrow. It's where we'll live after the wedding."

Maggie didn't say anything for a moment then reached out and covered Angie's hand with her own. "I hope you're not disappointed with the place. It's a little rough."

"What do you mean, rough?" Angie's stomach knotted.

"Well, I'm sure it probably just needs a woman's touch."

"Oookay, I'm not sure what that means, but I guess I'll see tomorrow. Tell me, Maggie, what do you know about Robert Beekman?"

Maggie stood and went over to wipe the counter again. "Not much."

"Tell me what you do know."

"I've heard he's a regular at the saloon." Maggie turned around to face Angie, her eyes filled with concern. "I heard he gets in fights a lot when he's there, and that he's pretty much a loner. That's about it."

A cold dread settled in the pit of Angie's stomach. She had a bad feeling about this arrangement. The man sounded as different from Marcus as one could be.

Forget about Marcus, she ordered herself. Marcus wasn't about to come riding in on a white horse and save her from wedding Robert Beekman. She'd gotten herself into this mess, now she was going to have to get herself out of it.

"Maybe he just needs a woman to calm him down," Maggie said hopefully. "Maybe he's ready to settle down and have a family."

"That's likely it. He did send for me, after all," Angie said hopefully.

"Right, and why would he do that if he wasn't ready for a wife?"

"I guess I'll just have to wait and see." She breathed a deep sigh. "You know, Maggie, I am exhausted from the trip. I think I'll go on up to bed."

"Well, of course, you are. I'm sorry I kept you up. Sweet dreams, Angie."

"Good night. See you tomorrow."

She went to her room and slipped out of her dress and into a long, white nightgown. She pulled the pins from her hair and sat on the bed while she brushed the fiery lengths, thoughts racing through her mind. She didn't think she could go through with this. Robert Beekman was not a man she wanted to spend the rest of her life with. He was at least ten years older than her, and on top of that, he was a drinker.

Memories of her father after he'd been drinking brought back ugly recollections. He yelled a lot, and sometimes he struck her. He'd take the money they needed for food and spend it at the tavern. She remembered many a night she'd gone to bed hungry and cried herself to sleep.

It was a terrible childhood, and she didn't want to spend her adulthood living through it again. Unfortunately, it sounded like that was the path she was on.

Maybe she shouldn't rush to judgment. Maybe he just made a bad first impression on people.

But it wasn't Maggie's first impression, Angie reminded herself. She'd lived here for years, and she seemed to have a bad taste in her mouth when she spoke about Robert Beekman. She'd tried to take a hopeful outlook, but Angie wasn't convinced. After all, you couldn't transform a hand-hooked rug into a Persian carpet just by wishing it were so.

She felt as if an icy fist was gripping her intestines. Fear wrapped around her like a blanket. Good Lord, what was she to do?

CHAPTER 7

Angie was ready the next morning when Robert Beekman came to pick her up. She tried to be optimistic as they rode in his wagon. It wasn't a buggy, by any means, but it got the job done.

Angie had to admit, it was beautiful here. The sky shimmered above, lazy white clouds puffing across its surface. Snowcapped mountains scraped the skyline and acres of green stretched for miles.

"Ya always got to be on the lookout when you're out here," Robert said. "Ya never know when you might come across a bear or a mountain lion. That's one of the first things we'll do is teach you to shoot."

The thought of shooting an animal made Angie cringe, but she tried to ignore it. It sounded like learning to shoot really was something she needed to do if she was going to live out here in the wild west. She shuddered at the image of being face to face with an angry grizzly.

"Yep, and of course, there are wolves and moose, all kinds of critters. Ya got to always be on your toes to survive out here. Heck, there could even be some Injuns on the warpath, ya never know." Robert continued to talk as they crossed a bridge over a deep ravine.

He certainly knows how to make a girl comfortable. Angie squirmed on the hard seat as she listened to his warnings.

"How much farther to the ranch?" Angie asked.

"It's probably another mile or two. We're not too far out from town. Just about five miles. This is our turn off here." He guided the horses around the corner, and they started going up a steep hill.

Angie clutched the seat as they jounced across the rough road, tall pines lining the way. It had rained hard here yesterday or the day before because the ruts were full of water, with mud splashing every step the horses took. It didn't seem to bother Robert. He just cracked the whip and yelled obscenities at the horses when they floundered.

"It's just on the other side of this rise," Robert informed her.

Anticipation transformed into dread when Angie caught sight of the shabby cabin before her. The porch sagged in the middle and the wind blew a loose shutter that banged against the house. A big hound dog lazed on the porch and barely lifted an eye when they approached. A few scraggly chickens walked across the bare ground, scratching for food, and a steer bellowed from the dilapidated barn.

"That there's Jethro," Robert said, indicating the dog. "He won't harm ya none. Come on, I'll show you the inside."

Angie climbed down from the buggy and stretched her aching back. She wanted to rub her sore behind, too, but she couldn't do it in front of Robert. She made her way carefully across the sagging porch as Robert threw open the door.

Inside was just as bad as she feared. It was one big room with hooks on the walls and a gray, dusty floor. Very little light came into the room through the small windows and a table sat in the middle of the floor. Dishes were scattered across its battered surface.

"Ya might want to do a little cleaning up before ya move in," he said. "It's just me here, and I haven't had time to fix it up."

Angie silently agreed but just said, "Well, there's no time like the present to get started."

"Yeah, you do that, and I'm going to go out to the barn. Be back for lunch."

Lunch? How was she supposed to fix lunch? There wasn't a clean dish in the house.

She made a quick trip to the creek out back and lugged water to the wood stove to heat. She gathered the dishes scattered across the cupboards and the table, trying not to think about the dreary situation. She was lucky to find a clean rag to wash the dishes and made quick work of it. The amount of crud on the table disgusted her and she scrubbed extra hard to remove it. Then she was determined to wash the curtain-less windows so she could see through them better. There were only two so that didn't take long, either. She swept the floor, whipping up so much dust it made her cough.

Now what to do about lunch, she wondered. She looked through the cabinets and managed to find some canned peaches, and there was a basket with a few eggs in it on the counter. There was enough bread to slice for toast. Well, he hadn't bothered to tell her where to find any meat, so breakfast for lunch it would be then.

Robert came in the door a few minutes later and whistled in appreciation. "Now ain't that nice? You done cleaned everything up."

"Well, not everything," she said, tossing a rueful gaze around at the unmade bed and some dirty clothes piled in the corner. "Are scrambled eggs fine with you?"

"Why, sure, little lady, scrambled eggs will do just fine," he said jovially. "Make enough for both of us now."

Angie tossed him a scathing look over her shoulder, but he wasn't paying attention to her, reaching for his cup of coffee instead. Did he really think she wasn't going to cook enough for both of them? After all, she'd worked hard cleaning up this pigsty.

She scraped the eggs onto the plates she'd just washed and added toast before setting them down on the table. She took her seat and watched him dig in.

He still wore his hat and hunkered over his plate like someone might try to take it from him. He shoveled eggs into his mouth, not noticing when some fell onto his lap. He slathered butter on his toast and then shoved nearly half a slice into his mouth.

She'd watched the Donahues enough to know that his table manners were atrocious. Goodness, just plain common sense said you shouldn't chew with your mouth open or smack your lips, but it didn't seem to bother him at all.

When every last crumb was consumed, Robert pushed himself back from the table, scratched his belly, and let out a loud belch. "Mmm, that was tasty."

"I'm glad you liked it," she managed to say with a straight face. "I'll just wash these dishes up, and then we should probably go back to town, don't you think?"

"What's the rush, little missy? You're gonna be my wife in less than a month, ain't ya? Now that I think on it, I don't see no reason why we have to wait for you to move in."

Angie collected the two plates and the two cups and carried them to the sink. "That wasn't the agreement, Mr. Beekman."

"Call me Bob, everybody does. Besides, it's costing me a fortune to keep you at that fancy boarding house. Why don't we just go back and get your stuff, then you can come stay here?"

She heard him approaching her from behind and stiffened when his meaty hands dropped on her shoulders.

"I said no, Mr. Beekman. Not until we're married."

"Ah, dumpling, you don't have to be shy with me. I want me a passel of sons, so we might as well get started."

Angie nearly screamed when she felt his hot breath on her neck. His lips slid across the soft skin there, and he ran his hands down her arms and back up again.

Angie whirled and pushed him away. "Stop! Don't touch me!"

Anger flashed across Robert's face, his mouth forming an ugly sneer. "All right, dolly, I'll let you off this time, but I expect you to be a whole lot more cooperative come our wedding night. You better be worth the big bucks I'm putting out."

"I'm sure you'll get what you paid for. Now, take me home, please."

"I'll hitch up the horses. You better be ready by the time I get back."

Angie watched him go as she fought back tears. How could she even consider marrying this man?

CHAPTER 8

The ride back was made in near silence. Angie clung to her side of the seat and sucked in her breath every time the rough ride bounced her into Robert. She didn't want to be near him. She breathed a sigh of relief when they pulled up in front of Maggie's house.

Angie climbed down from the wagon unassisted again and was almost to the porch when Robert called out to her.

"Hey, don't forget there's a barn dance Saturday night. I'll be around to pick ya up."

Angie nodded and made her way into the house. Maggie was dusting the parlor when Angie walked in and soon sensed something was wrong.

"Come here and sit down and tell Aunt Maggie all about it," she said, patting the seat of the chair next to her. "Would you like some lemonade?"

"That sounds good, Maggie. Thanks." Angie settled back and waited on her return, twisting the braided handles of her reticule the entire time. Maggie was back in just a few moments and handed Angie a glass of cold beverage.

"Now I know something's wrong. I can tell by the look on your face. What is it?"

Angie didn't really know how to explain her misgivings about Bob Beekman. Besides, she'd gotten herself into this fix, it should be up to her to get out of it. It wasn't Angie's problem. Instead, she led with the next problem that was bothering her.

"It's nothing, really. It's just that Bob mentioned there was a dance Saturday night, and and I don't have anything to wear. All my clothes are old and faded. I just don't want to make a bad first impression on the town folks."

"Is that all? Oh, honey, I've got a half a dozen= dresses upstairs that are too little for me." She patted her still small waistline. "I've put on a few pounds over the years. You're welcome to all of them. I'll even help you alter them if they need it."

"Would you? I don't want to put you out or take advantage of you."

"Now, I don't want to hear another word about it. I was thinking about finding someone they'd fit and giving them away anyhow. Why shouldn't I give them to you? They're just going to waste up there in my wardrobe. Come on, I'll show them to you."

Maggie led the way, her excitement contagious. By the time they reached the room Maggie shared with Katie, they were giggling like schoolgirls.

"You sit on the bed. Let me get the dresses," Maggie ordered, turning around to rummage in the closet. The first dress she pulled out was a serviceable blue-and-white checkered cotton and Angie stroked her hand across the soft fabric. These dresses which Maggie called work dresses were better than anything she had ever owned. There was also a green dress, a yellow, and a navy blue. Two dresses especially caught her eye. They were a little dressier, one made of a beautiful lavender fabric with lilacs embroidered on the collar, and the other was light orange with ruffles around the hem.

"Oh, Maggie, these are too fine. I can't accept them."

"Oh, yes you can, and you will," Maggie commanded. "I really don't fit them anymore."

"I've never had such fine clothes. Should I try one on?"

"I think it will need hemming so come on downstairs when you're dressed, and I'll mark the hem."

Angie took a moment to whisper a prayer of gratitude that she at least had Maggie here. She missed Tilly, and her heart ached for Marcus. She knew she and Maggie were becoming close friends and that helped ease her loneliness.

She slipped on the checkered dress and ran her hands across the waistline. It fit perfectly other than it was just a little too long. She knew she was going to sit down and write Tilly a letter tonight about how good and kind Maggie was—surely Tilly could find someone to read it to her. She wasn't sure if she would tell her feelings about Bob Beekman or not. If she did, it would be the perfect opportunity for Tilly to say, "I told you so," and Angie wouldn't blame her.

It wasn't that she didn't like it here in Fort Regent. She had to admit she loved the quiet. Boston was always a cacophony of noise. Carts and wagons always rumbling by, vendors hawking their wares, and all the other sounds of the city filled the air, and there was little tranquility to be found.

The problem was Bob Beekman. He was pushy, rude, and uncouth. Even some of the beggar boys on the streets of Boston were well mannered enough to say thank you when someone did something for them. She had a terrible feeling that life as his wife was going to be nothing but work and discomfort, not to mention embarrassing if he treated everyone as he had treated her so far.

Well, Maggie was waiting. She didn't have time to worry about Bob's manners now.

She went downstairs and found Maggie in the parlor. Kevin and Katie had come home from school while she was in her room. Kevin had grabbed his cane pole and said he was going fishing with his friend Caleb, but Katie had curled up on a chair in the parlor. She plied Angie with questions while Angie stood and turned occasionally so Maggie could pin the hem.

Katie sat and listened, enthralled, as Angie talked about the ocean, the stores, and the mansion she had worked in.

"It sounds wonderful. Tell me, why would anyone ever want to leave such a place to come to a little town like Fort Regent?"

The question caught Angie by surprise. She didn't really know how to answer it. She didn't think she could tell this young girl the truth, that she had been fraternizing with her employer's son and gotten herself fired. That she hadn't had a choice but to become a stranger's bride if she wanted to continue eating without prostituting herself.

Fortunately, Maggie stepped in and saved her. "Now, Katie, it's rude to ask such personal questions. You go in and start peeling potatoes for supper now. You can talk more to Angie later."

The little girl looked abashed, and then muttered an apology to Angie before she slunk out of the room.

"I'm sorry, Angie. She's just so excited about meeting someone from the big city, she forgot her manners."

"I don't blame her for being curious."

No, I blame myself for getting in this position. Selling herself. Wasn't that what she was doing, only to just one man instead of a variety. Her stomach roiled at the thought of Bob Beekman touching her again. If only it was Marcus Donahue she was going to wed, she would be looking forward to consummating the wedding, not dreading it like she was being sent to the gallows.

CHAPTER 9

Angie worked on hemming the first dress that night, and the next day, she and Maggie worked together to do two more of them. Angie decided to wear the lavender dress with embroidered lilacs on it to the dance. She was looking forward to going. She wasn't expecting to enjoy Bob Beekman's company, but she'd appreciate meeting some of the other people who lived in the area. If she was going to live here, she would probably need all the friends she could get.

She helped Maggie with the housework each day and then escaped to the front porch with a book Maggie had lent her. She was amazed by how easily the words were beginning to flow, and she got completely caught up in the story of a young girl whose parents forced her to move across the country and leave the love of her life. Angie cried as she read it. It was a tragic love story much like her own.

It was during quiet moments like this, as she sat rocking back and forth in the swing on the front porch, that she missed Marcus the most. The gentle breeze seemed to carry the memory of his voice and the touch of his lips on hers. She could almost feel the softness of his hair beneath her fingers. She loved to wrap the silky locks around her finger.

She missed him so badly it was like a constant drumbeat, hammering away at her heart. She'd cried herself to sleep the last two nights in a row, soaking her pillow with tears. *Just another foolish thing to do,* Angie derided herself. Tears weren't going to help her now.

The dance was this evening. She supposed she should go get ready. She was looking forward to wearing her new dress and meeting new people. She hadn't had much chance to venture out and explore the town.

She was ready when Bob came to pick her up. She'd swept her chestnut hair up on top of her head, and Maggie gave her a little bow of lavender satin to wear tucked in her curls. The dress fit like it had been made for her, and Angie actually felt pretty. She'd never had that feeling before. She ran her hands down the soft fabric that was so different from the faded, thin dresses she was used to wearing.

Bob didn't bother to compliment her on how she looked when he came to pick her up, but Angie hadn't thought he would. He wasn't the type that noticed much about other people.

"Bye, Maggie. We'll see you all there," Angie called out as they left. Maggie had told her that everyone in town went to these affairs, and she and the children would be there. Maggie felt relief that she would know at least someone besides Bob at the dance.

The barn where the dance was being held was on the outskirts of town. Horses and a variety of conveyances were parked in front of the barn that glowed with light. Angie caught the twang of music as she climbed out of the wagon, and her spirits picked up when she heard the beat.

When they walked in, Bob holding proprietarily to her elbow, Angie noticed the band along the back wall. She recognized Mr. Little, her fellow boarder, playing the fiddle and grinning merrily. Two men with guitars played along, and a caller hollered out the steps. Some folks danced, others gathered around the refreshment table, and still others sat on bales of hay around the edge of the barn, chatting and visiting together. A couple of kids chased each other across the room with a little one toddling after them.

Angie felt her toes begin to tap to the rhythm of the band and turned an expectant face towards Bob. Surely, he'd want to dance. That was why they came.

Much to her surprise, though, he guided her towards a hay bale and told her to sit.

"I'll be back," he said and headed across the room toward a group of other cowboys. Angie couldn't believe he'd basically dumped her on a hay bale in a barn where she didn't know another soul and walked away.

She was still fuming when Maggie and her kids came into the barn. Maggie spotted Angie and headed her way. Kevin and Katie each headed toward a group of their friends.

"Hi, Angie," Maggie greeted her, taking a seat on the adjacent hay bale. "Where's Mr. Beekman?"

Angie shrugged. "He plopped me here and took off as soon as we got here."

Maggie couldn't conceal the flash of anger that quickly swept across her face even though she clearly tried.

"Well, don't you worry, Angie. You're going to have a good time this evening. Everybody dances with everybody, and there are lots of friendly folks here. Let me introduce you to some of them now." She stood and started walking toward a group of ladies and Angie followed.

Angie was relieved to find Maggie was right. Everybody was friendly, and Angie soon found herself on the dance floor with Maggie's other border, Cecil James. Then another old gentleman became Angie's partner. Even Kevin took a turn whirling her around the floor.

Angie wound up partnered with a tall, lanky young man named Zeke Taylor. Angie thought he was about seventeen years old, and she loved the way he blushed every time he talked to her. When he asked her if she wanted some punch, she readily agreed. Dancing turned out to be hot work.

Zeke was coming back with two cups of punch when Bob Beekman suddenly decided to reappear. His face wore an angry scowl as he strode to where Angie stood.

"So, I hear you're the belle of the ball," he snarled, grabbing her elbow. "They tell me you've been dancing up a storm out here."

"Maggie said everyone dances with each other, so that's what I was doing." She tried to pull away from the smell of alcohol coming from his breath.

"Well, you're my girl. I don't want you dancing with everybody else. Now you're gonna dance with me."

"Here's your punch, Angie," Zeke said holding out a glass to her as he returned.

Bob whirled around at the sound of his voice and yelled, "Punch! You say you want a punch. Well, have one."

With that, he doubled up his fist and smacked Zeke right in the nose.

CHAPTER 10

Angie lay in bed that night with tears silently streaking down her cheeks. She couldn't believe the mess she'd gotten herself into, and worse yet, she didn't know how to get out of it.

Scenes from this evening's fiasco kept playing through her mind. She saw Bob punch Zeke over and over again though, in reality, he'd only hit him once. Zeke reeled and fell to the floor. Blood gushed from his nose and punch drenched his shirt. Ladies screamed, and men began to shout. It was a scene from a nightmare.

Angie had been so angry with Bob that she had refused to let him take her home. He reacted badly to that and stormed off, leaving her at the barn dance. That was fine with her. She didn't want to spend any more time with him than was absolutely necessary.

Maggie and the kids walked home with Angie. Angie managed to control her tears during the walk, but once they'd gotten home and the kids went to bed, Angie broke down and cried on Maggie's shoulder.

"Ah, Maggie, I've made a deal with the devil," she sobbed.

"I think Bob Beekman *is* the devil," Maggie growled. "I can't let you marry that man. That would be torture for you."

"I don't know how to get out of it," Angie wailed. "The contract says if I don't go through with it, I'll be responsible for everything spent sending me out here."

"Don't worry, Angie. We'll think of something. If only you had family or a friend that could help you out."

"I don't have anyone, Maggie, not a soul in the world. Well, there's…" She broke off before she confessed about Marcus.

"Who is it, Angie? Is it someone who has the means to help?"

She nodded reluctantly then let the whole story about Marcus come out.

"You need to write to him, Angie. Do it right now," Maggie pleaded. "I'll bet he'll help you."

Angie shook her head stubbornly. "No. I'm not going to confess to him what a mess I've made of things. Besides, if his parents ever found out he was helping me, they'd disown him."

Maggie continued to argue, but Angie remained resolute. It wouldn't do any good to turn to Marcus. Even if he was at home, how could he help from the other side of the country? No, this was a problem she was going to have to resolve herself.

Now, she lay in bed with tears rolling down her face. She wasn't sobbing anymore, but she couldn't seem to stop the waterworks coming from her eyes.

She rolled on her side and wadded the damp pillow up beneath her head and considered her options. There wasn't much to consider. The only choice she felt she had was to run away, but she had no idea where to go or how to get there. She didn't have any money for train fare or a stagecoach ticket. She didn't even have much left for food besides a little of the remaining stipend she'd been given.

Fear and confusion warred over which would take over her mind first. She didn't know what to do and the more she thought about it, the worse her options seemed.

Finally, exhaustion took over, and she fell into a troubled sleep.

Angie awoke the next morning with a throbbing headache, aching, burning eyes, and a new determination. She'd had an epiphany during the night. Maybe Bob wasn't any happier with this arrangement than she was. She needed to talk to him about it and see if they could work something out. Maybe he'd let her pay him back his expenses over time.

She wanted to talk the idea over with Maggie but had trouble catching a minute alone with her. It didn't happen until after lunch. They finished the dishes, and Katie asked to go to a friend's house. After she left, Angie and Maggie headed to the porch for a break and a glass of cold tea.

"It looks like you're feeling a little better this afternoon," Maggie said as they settled into rocking chairs. "Did you get any sleep at all last night?"

"Not much." Angie shrugged. "Every time I closed my eyes, I kept seeing Bob punching Zeke in the face."

"I know, but thank goodness Zeke will be okay, even if he does have a swollen honker for a while."

Angie nodded sympathetically and murmured, "I know, and Zeke is such a nice young man, too. I can't believe Bob thought there might be something going on between us. I had a thought."

"What's that?"

"What if I just talk to Robert and ask him to release me from the contract? What's the worst that can happen?" She leaned forward in her earnestness.

"Well, he could say no." Maggie turned her hands up in a questionable gesture.

"He won't, though. He can't," she said desperately. "I can't marry him."

Maggie looked doubtful. After all, it was Bob Beekman they were talking about. "I pray he's agreeable to the idea."

Angie nodded, a worried look on her face, and Maggie reached over and covered Angie's hands with her own. "Don't worry, Angie. This will all work out somehow."

Angie's eyes grew wide and her face paled as she looked past Angie toward the street. "I guess I'll find out his answer soon. Here he comes."

Maggie turned around and saw the brawny man riding up on his horse. "Well, at least you'll get it over with quickly this way. I'll leave you two alone. Good luck."

Angie almost pleaded with her to stay, to not leave her alone with this awful man, but she resisted the temptation. They really didn't need an audience for this showdown.

Angie met him as he strode up the steps. He at least had the decency to look slightly abashed as he greeted her. "I wanted to make sure you got home all right last night."

Angie looked at him without smiling. "Well, you can see I did. Maggie and the kids walked me home."

"I'm sorry about that, Angie. I guess I had a little too much to drink, but that kid had it coming to him. You're my girl, and I don't want any young buck staking a claim on ya."

"Bob, that's ridiculous. Zeke is a teenager. I don't even think he shaves yet."

"Don't matter. They ain't never too young to learn."

Knowing she'd never convince him otherwise, Angie quickly changed the subject to what she wanted to talk about.

"Um, Bob, sit down, won't you? I want to talk to you."

Bob slouched into a rocker and Angie took a seat in the other one. "Bob, you know you and I are very different. I don't think we make a very good match. I think we should call off our engagement."

Angie waited silently as she watched the color mount in Bob's cheeks and a cold, menacing stare come into his eyes. She jerked when he slammed his hands on the arms of the rocker and lurched to his feet.

"Look, lady, as far as I'm concerned you are bought and paid for. You belong to me." He towered over her as he glared down at her. "Now I don't want to hear any more foolish talk about calling off our engagement."

"What if I pay you back what you spent on me so far? I could give you a couple of dollars down and then make payments on the rest. I'll get a job."

"That would take too long. I need you out at the ranch now. Now, I've heard enough. If you refuse to marry me, I'll make you pay the hard way." He smacked his beefy fist into the palm of his hand before striding off the porch and climbing on his horse.

Angie held a clenched fist to her lips as she stared after him as he rode away. What a horrible, beastly man. She couldn't possibly spend the rest of her life with him, but what was she to do?

There was only one thing she could do. She had to run away.

CHAPTER 11

Maggie came out and found Angie still sitting on the porch, her hands trembling and her face pale.

"I guess that didn't go well," Maggie said, and Angie laughed harshly.

"To say the least," she said in a strangled voice. "He insists we get married. I even offered to pay him back all of his expenses over time, but he scoffed at the idea. Said it would take too long. Oh, Maggie, I don't know what to do. I can't marry him. I just can't."

"I know, I know. We'll figure something out." She wrapped her arms around Angie and hugged her tight. "We'll put our heads together and think of something."

Angie wished she was as confident, but she knew there was no other way. She had to leave Fort Regent, and she had to do it right away. She didn't know how or where she would go, but she did know she needed to figure it out quickly.

She got an idea that night at supper when Mr. Little said he was taking a trip to a little town ten miles north where his son lived. Ten miles. That wasn't far. Maybe she could walk there. It couldn't take more than a day.

"Yep, it's a pretty little town straight down the road from here. I figure me and Jimmy will get in some fishing, and I'll spend some time playing with my grandkids. Can't wait to go next week."

Angie's mind was turning over quickly. Maybe when she got there, she could go to Jimmy Little's house and ask if anyone nearby needed to hire a woman for work.

At least, it was a whisper of hope. Maybe if she could hide out long enough, Bob Beekman would give up, or she could save up enough money to buy a ticket to someplace else

She wasn't going to tell anyone she was going. They would try to stop her, and she couldn't let that happen. She had to get away.

She didn't sleep much that night. She packed her carpetbag and set it by the door so it would be ready to go. She tried to sleep but nerves only allowed her to doze in short bursts, and then she would wake up with frightening thoughts running through her mind.

Finally, she decided it was time to go. The sun hadn't come up over the horizon yet, but she didn't want to waste any time. She wrapped a couple of leftover biscuits in a napkin and added an apple and a piece of fried chicken, then she wrote Maggie a note thanking her for her kindness and apologizing for taking the food.

She slipped out the door and stood on the sidewalk a moment and stared at the house. She would miss Maggie and the kids, but she couldn't stay here any longer. Determinedly, she started down the street heading north.

The first couple of hours weren't too bad. The full moon provided enough light for her to see as she made her way along the road. This was the opposite direction from Bob Beekman's ranch so that was a relief. At least, she probably wouldn't run into him on her way. She was more worried about encountering a bear or a mountain lion on the isolated road.

By the time the sun crept up over the horizon, Angie thought she had walked about two miles. The road was getting steeper and started winding upward through the mountains. Her legs were starting to ache with every step she took, but she was determined she was going to get to her destination today.

At first, the sun felt good on her back but eventually, it began to heat up and she was sweating profusely as she walked on. The road grew steeper and the woods on either side grew thicker. She saw squirrels and a fox, rabbits, and deer. If that was the only wildlife she encountered, she could deal with that.

Soon, though, thunderclouds came rolling in, and the wind died away. An eerie stillness seemed to fill the air, and Angie looked worriedly up at the sky. Rain would be falling momentarily, and she was going to get soaked.

That wasn't going to stop her, though. She had to go on. She didn't have anywhere to hide from the storm anyway.

She reached a spot in the road that seemed extra steep, and she had to work hard to get up the expanse. The hills rolled away on either side, and she shuddered. She'd hate to fall down there.

The first drops of rain splattered the ground and in seconds Angie was drenched. It was a cold rain, and it wasn't long before she was shivering. Lightning flared through the sky, and the loud crashes of thunder made her jump with every explosion.

She ducked under the overhanging branches of a towering pine tree and tried to protect herself from the rain.

Crouching low, she enjoyed the relative dryness of the space. When her stomach growled, she decided this was as good a place as any to have the apple she'd brought.

She crunched into the crispy flesh and was chewing when she heard a noise behind her. Whirling around, she peered into the dense foliage, her gaze darting from place to place. What was it she heard?

That's the moment lightning struck a tree about a hundred feet away. There was a huge boom and a flash of light that made her jump. Her feet slipped on the needles under the tree and then she was falling, rolling down the steep hill.

CHAPTER 12

Angie groaned as she lay on the ground curled up against the trunk of a tree. Stunned, she didn't move for a minute. Pain radiated from her ankle, and she'd hit her head on something hard like a rock or a tree limb.

Slowly, she managed to pull herself upright, but pain shot through her ankle when she tried to put weight on it. Goodness, now she was stuck out here, and every step would be agonizing. She fell back onto the ground and started to inch her way up the incline.

She had almost reached the top when she heard a horse galloping along the road. She needed help, and this might be her only chance. She hadn't seen another soul along the way. Who knew how long it would be before someone else came along? She grabbed a stick and used it to leverage herself to a standing position and turned her face hopefully toward the sound of the approaching horse.

Her stomach fell when she recognized the rider. It was Bob Beekman.

"So, this is where you ran off to. I figured you'd head to McClain Falls. It's the only other town around here. Well, come on up here. I'll take you back." Bob stuck out his hand to hoist her onto the horse, but she hesitated to take it. She didn't want to go anywhere with this man.

"Quit wasting time, woman," he barked. "Don't make me get off this horse and come get ya."

"I don't want to go with you, and I certainly don't want to marry you." She stuck out her chin in a stubborn manner and glared at him defiantly.

"Have it your way then. I'll just leave you out here all alone and go back to town. I think I'll pay a call on your friend Maggie. Maybe you'll be a little more…understanding…after I rough her up a little bit."

"You wouldn't dare touch her," Angie shouted. "You'll have the whole town after you."

"Yeah, I guess you're right. You need punished for leading me on and costing me money, though. Maybe I'll just sneak out at night and burn her house down with her and the kids in it. Would you like that?"

Angie drew back in horror at his suggestion. Would he actually go that far to get his revenge? The idea sickened her.

"You are a monster," she uttered scathingly, "but you're not leaving me any choice, are you?"

"Not really, sweetheart. Now climb on up here, and let's go."

She didn't want to do it. She wanted to run away as fast and as far as she could, but it wasn't possible. In the first place, she couldn't run anywhere with her sprained ankle, and most importantly, she didn't trust Bob not to follow through with his threat. What if he really did burn Maggie's house down?

Reluctantly, she reached up her hand and let Bob pull her up behind him on the horse. She cringed at his nearness and felt nauseous when his smell wafted to her nose. He smelled like old sweat and stale beer combined.

The wet ride back was made in silence. She didn't want to wrap her arms around his waist but she didn't have a choice. She'd never ridden astride a horse before and felt like she was far above the earth. Every jounce sent pain spiraling through her ankle, and her head was aching. She couldn't throw off the air of sadness that weighed her down. Now, not only was she in trouble, she'd brought danger to Maggie and the kids. Lord, if anything happened to them, she would never forgive herself.

Bob pulled up in front of the boarding house and pulled her down from the horse. She winced as her foot touched the ground, hopping a bit to avoid putting weight on it.

"Listen here, girlie," Bob growled, glancing up at the house. "Don't forget what I said about your friend Maggie. It'd be a shame if such a nice place went up in flames."

Angie shook her head. "Don't worry. I won't forget."

"See you don't. Remember, our wedding's in less than two weeks. You better show up at the church."

She nodded and hoisted her bag in her arms then turned and hobbled away from him. She felt his gaze on her all the way up the walk.

Maggie looked up in surprise when Angie walked in. "Angie? Oh, Angie, I've been so worried about you."

"I'm okay. I was going to run away, but I didn't get very far."

"Sit down and tell me what happened. Are you limping? Here, let me get you some tea."

Angie took a seat at the kitchen table and proceeded to tell Maggie her story. She was careful to leave out the part about Bob's threats to burn the house down. Maggie didn't deserve to have that kind of worry thrown at her.

"Oh, you must be worn out. Is your ankle very painful? Let me get some cloth and wrap it up for you."

Angie glanced down at herself and realized what a mess she was. Her still damp hair strung around her face, and there were mud and grass stains across her skirt. Her hands were dirty and had scratches on them from the rocks and briars she'd encountered. Exhaustion washed over her.

"I-I think I'll go upstairs and get cleaned up. When I come down, I'll help get supper."

"You aren't helping with anything with that ankle of yours. Why don't you take a little nap while you're up there? You look plum worn out."

Angie nodded and made her way up the stairs. She sat on the edge of the bed, her shoulders slumped. Things were hopeless. She could see no way out of her situation without endangering her friends.

What would life with a man like Bob Beekman be like? A man who would threaten to burn down someone's house with them inside simply because he didn't get his own way? She was heading into a living nightmare, and there was no way to stop the journey.

CHAPTER 13

Angie spent the next few days being babied by Maggie and Katie. Angie was placed in the most comfortable chair and had her foot propped on a pillow on top of a stool. She read books and ate the treats Maggie was always bringing her.

Angie insisted on helping with what she could. She peeled potatoes, chopped vegetables, and did other tasks that Maggie allowed her to do. Maggie lent her a walking stick that had belonged to her father, so Angie was able to hobble around the house and accomplish some things.

She was in the middle of peeling apples for a pie when Maggie asked what she had decided to do about the wedding.

Angie's face didn't change expression. She didn't want to tell Maggie about Bob's threats, so she kept a solemn façade and concentrated on wielding the paring knife.

"I've decided to go through with it," she said calmly. "I'm going to marry Bob Beekman next Saturday."

Maggie tried to conceal a little breath she sucked in, but Angie heard it. She knew what Maggie was going to say.

"You … you are?" Maggie asked doubtfully.

"Yes. I don't have any other options. Besides, I will have a roof over my head which is more than what I had back in Boston."

"Yes, but Angie, it's *Bob Beekman*. Do you honestly think you can live with that man?" Maggie fretted, her face looking aghast.

"I'll have to. I don't have a choice." Angie swallowed and tried to keep the waver from her voice. "I can't go back to Boston and be homeless. I can't ask Marcus for help—he'd lose everything. I came out here to find security, to have a home. I will at least accomplish that goal."

"But, Angie, that doesn't mean you'll be happy."

"I'll make my own happiness. I'll enjoy the beautiful scenery, and I'll learn to ride a horse. I'll have a garden and plenty of food. It will work out. Please don't worry about me."

"You're my friend. Of course, I'm going to worry about you."

Angie blinked back tears at her words. "I can't tell you what that means to me. I've never had many friends."

"Oh, Ang," Maggie wailed and hugged her tightly. "I just want you to be happy."

"I know, Maggie, I know." Angie sobbed. She couldn't help it. Emotion overwhelmed her. Tilly was the only other friend Angie had ever had and to have this sweet, refined woman so concerned touched Angie deeply. She knew she would do what she had to do to protect her.

"Angie, what will you do if Bob turns out to be abusive? You know he has a hair-trigger temper. You saw what he did to Zeke." Maggie's face showed her distress.

"I'm a woman. He surely won't hit me," Angie lied. She figured he wouldn't care if she was female or not. Well, her father had hit her regularly throughout her childhood. She guessed she could stand up for herself if she had to. Maybe she would keep a cast iron skillet close at hand all the time in case she had to defend herself.

"Well," Angie said as she pulled back and smiled, "These apples aren't going to peel themselves and magically turn into a pie. I better finish up."

Maggie nodded, swiping at her tears and returning Angie's smile. "Yes, and I need to change the bed linens. I better get to work. And it's not too late to change your mind. I'll help you. You can stay here for free."

Angie lowered her lashes and took a deep breath. She only wished she could accept that kind invitation, but fear stopped her. Even if Maggie and the children survived, a fire would be devastating. It could take everything from them.

"Thank you, but I am going to marry Bob Beekman."

"If you have to." Maggie sighed and left the room shaking her head.

Angie knew Maggie didn't understand why she now said she would marry Bob, but there was no way she was going to tell her. Maggie would get angry and probably would confront Bob and make him even angrier. It was not like Fort Regent actually had a marshal to report him to. Angie might have considered doing that if there was any kind of law here, but there wasn't.

She finished making the pie, then made her way up to her room. She wanted to write Tilly again, and she thought she might lie down and try to nap. She hadn't been sleeping well at night.

Angie sat in the little rocker next to the open window and stared out over the little town, her mind lost in thought. She couldn't help dwelling on her future. It looked bleak, like a lifetime of work with no rewards. She dreaded moving into the ramshackle cabin. The only thing she thought she would enjoy was the scenery.

She did love the wide-open spaces of Wyoming. You could see for miles from the hilltops, and the vistas fascinated her. Rivers flowed and rippled through the countryside, and giant boulders massed in unique formations.

She compared this wild countryside with Boston and knew Boston lost. Yes, there were parts of the city that were beautiful, but there were other parts where trash blew through the gutters, and tumble-down cottages lined the streets. When it snowed, it was beautiful at first but within a couple of days, the lovely white velvety coat covering the earth turned gray and slushy.

She would have missed the serenity of this place if she had returned to the noisy hustle and bustle of Boston. She loved getting up in the morning and taking her coffee out on the porch and listening to the birds sing or going for a walk along a country lane. It offered her an inner peace she'd been missing in the city. Maybe she could get enough of that out at the ranch. It did sit on a beautiful piece of property.

Yes, but the problem was the property came attached to Bob Beekman. She didn't think she would be able to feel serenity when Bob was involved. She would probably be too busy cooking and cleaning to take any time for tranquility. Despite what she had told Maggie, she didn't believe she'd ever find happiness married to the rude, obnoxious man.

CHAPTER 14

Despite the fact that she'd been hoping to be struck by lightning or suffer some other natural disaster to prevent her from having to go through with this marriage, her wedding day had arrived.

Angie almost found it an insult that the morning dawned bright and sunny. It would have been more appropriate if it had been raining and the sky gray and overcast. It would have matched her mood.

She lingered in bed for longer than usual, reluctant to get ready to go to the church. Even though Fort Regent didn't have a full-time minister, the citizens had banded together to build a church in hopes that they soon would get a preacher to live here. In the meantime, it was used as a school.

Angie rolled over on her side, not even conscious that tears rolled silently down her face. How sad that she felt like this on the day she was to be married. Girls dreamed of their wedding days from the time they were little, but it felt like hers had turned into a nightmare.

She dreaded her future life, but even more, she was terrified of that night. How could she possibly stand Bob touching her, his blubbery lips kissing her? It would take sheer force of will to keep her from screaming and running from the room.

When she knew she could put it off no longer, she crawled from bed and got dressed in everyday clothes for now. She wouldn't dress for the wedding until after breakfast.

Maggie studied her intently when she walked into the kitchen. Angie did her best to smile and act happy, but she knew she wasn't fooling her friend.

"Here, Angie, sit down. I've made breakfast for us. I thought maybe you and I might like to eat out here in the kitchen instead of with the others. That way we can have some girl talk."

Maggie slid a couple of fried eggs on each plate and poured them both mugs of coffee before she sat down to join Angie.

"It's a beautiful day for a wedding," Maggie said as she bit into a slice of bacon.

"Yes, it's lovely." Angie idly ran her fork through her eggs, not really feeling like eating.

"I need to know. Are you sure about this? It's not too late to change your mind."

Angie swallowed deeply. She so wanted to tell Maggie the truth, to scream out her refusal to go through with this. She wanted to act like a child and throw a tantrum, stamping her feet and flailing her fists.

But she wasn't a child. As the old saying went, she'd made her bed, now she had to lie in it. Most importantly, she couldn't take the chance Bob would carry out his threats.

"I'm touched that you care so much, but I'm going to do this." She managed to keep her voice steady despite the twisting of her guts. She even made herself look steadily into Maggie's eyes without crying.

"Well, I want you to know you can come back here anytime. I mean it. If you ever need someplace to go, come to me. Promise." Maggie looked so earnest that Angie almost sobbed out loud.

"I promise. I don't think it will ever come to that, but I will always remember your offer." Angie smiled warmly at Maggie and reached over and hugged her. "Now, I think I better go and get ready. It won't be long until I'm a married woman."

"That's right. I need to get ready, too. I guess we better get started." Maggie stood from the table and gathered their breakfast dishes and carried them to the sink. "You go on up, and I'll be up as soon as I finish these dishes. It will just take me a minute."

Angie offered to stay and help, but Maggie shooed her off. Angie went upstairs dragging her feet. She was in no hurry to get to the church. She felt more like she was preparing for the gallows rather than her wedding. If there could only be a miracle…

She sat on the edge of the bed and brushed her hair while she tried to give herself a pep talk. She would do what she had to do. She was strong and would get through this. She had endured much in her life, and she would survive this as well.

She caught sight of her image in the mirror. Her face was pale and waxen-looking, surrounded by her long, flowing auburn curls. Her green eyes looked huge in her face, opened wide with violet circles underneath the orbs. The freckles scattered across her nose stood out like brown polka dots on a white dress.

Maybe people would put down her appearance to just bridal jitters. Hopefully, there wouldn't be many people there, though Maggie had warned her the whole town usually showed up for all the marry-ings and bury-ings, as she put it.

Finally, Angie knew she could put it off no longer. She had to get dressed for the wedding. After she pinned her hair up, she slipped into the coral-colored dress with the ruffle along the hem. Maggie had picked some flowers to put in Angie's hair, and now she slipped in the lilies-of-the-valleys in her copper locks. She was ready.

Angie squared her shoulders and went down the stairs. Maggie and Katie must still be getting ready. She didn't see them anywhere down here. She headed to the parlor to wait for them.

She had just stepped through the pocket doors into the room when a knock on the door startled her. *Who is it,* she wondered, fearing it would be Bob himself. She moved to the door and swung it open.

When she saw who stood on the other side of the door, she thought she was seeing things. She blinked a few times, trying to clear her vision. No, the image hadn't changed. She wasn't dreaming.

Marcus Donahue stood on the doorstep.

CHAPTER 15

A wave of faintness came over Angie even as she reached out to touch him and make sure he was real. A roaring started in her head, and she felt her knees buckle.

"Angie," Marcus cried out as he scooped her up in his arms and headed toward the sofa. "Angel, it's me, Marcus."

"Is it really you?" she whispered, laying the palm of her hand against his cheek. Yes, it was warm, real. "Dear God, Marcus, it is you."

"Yes, my darling. Am I in time? Are you married yet?"

Angie sat up and cupped her forehead. This wasn't happening. She had to be dreaming.

"No, I'm not married yet. But I am on my way to the church to get married. Oh, Marcus, I don't want to marry Bob Beekman, but I have to."

Marcus's cheeks grew pale, and he clutched her arms. "Angie, you're not…"

It dawned on her what he meant, and she almost laughed. "No, I'm not with child."

She went on to explain her predicament, twisting her fingers as she spoke.

"And, Marcus, I'm so afraid. What if he follows through on his threats? What if he burns Maggie's house down?"

Marcus gathered her in his arms and held her close. He dropped a kiss on the top of her head and stroked her cheek.

"Is that all you're worried about? Darling, that's an easy fix. If I know the type of man Bob Beekman is, I can easily buy him off."

"Angie? Who are you talking to? We've got to get going or you'll be late for your own wedding," Maggie warned as she walked into the room. Her eyes widened at the sight that met her eyes. Angie was propped up on the couch in a strange man's arms.

Angie looked at her dear friend. "Maggie, I want you to meet Marcus Donahue. You remember I told you about him?"

Maggie's face instantly relaxed into a smile. "What? Is it so? Marcus Donahue of Boston?"

"Yes, ma'am," Marcus said, rising to his feet.

"Have you come to save the day?"

"I hope so. I aim to marry Angie myself." He looked down at Angie, his blue eyes burning like blue flames. "I love her very much."

Angie drew in a sharp breath. He'd told her that once before, and she had dared to believe him. Hearing it again, made her eyes fill with tears. "You…you love me?"

"Of course, I do. You know that. Tilly didn't want to tell me where you were, but I finally convinced her I needed to find you, to beg you not to marry someone else."

Angie barely noticed Maggie slip from the room, her eyes trained solely on Marcus. She ran her gaze over his expression, so serious, so sincere, and felt joy building in her heart. He was here, she could touch him, kiss him.

Laughter suddenly bubbled out of her. "Marcus, I love you, too. I've missed you so much I could hardly stand it. I can't believe you're really here."

"Maybe this will help convince you." He lowered his head and his lips captured hers. Angie moaned and wrapped her hands around his neck, delving her fingers into his silky, coffee-colored locks, pulling him closer and treasuring the taste of his sweet kiss.

"Y-you taste too good to be real," she sighed into his mouth. "You have to be a dream, and I hope I never wake up."

"Say you'll marry me, angel. Please be my wife and spend the rest of your life with me."

Joy exploded through her then suddenly, it popped like a balloon. "I want to Marcus, but your parents. They'll disown you."

"Don't worry about that. I have enough money to get by without them. At least, to start us out. Besides, if I know George and Agatha Donahue, they'll come round eventually."

"Y-you'd give up your inheritance for me?"

"In a heartbeat," he assured her, snuggling her neck. "Now, let's go break the news to your ex-fiancé."

"Ex-fiancé. Those are the most beautiful words I've ever heard."

Angie and Marcus walked to the church near the center of town and entered the building together. Bob Beekman stood at the front of the church, an impatient look on his face. When he saw her walk in with Marcus, his expression darkened.

"It's about time you showed up, missy. Who's this yahoo anyway?"

Marcus stepped up and stuck out his hand. "I'm Marcus Donahue, Mr. Beekman. I want to make a deal with you."

Suspicion immediately leapt into Beekman's eyes. "What kind of deal? What are you talking about?"

"You look like a man who likes to make a fast buck. How would you like five hundred of them?"

Bob's eyes bulged in his face. "Five hundred dollars? What do I have to do?"

"Don't marry Miss Rosewood here. That's it." Marcus shrugged. "And, of course, don't ever harm her or Maggie's house or family. Don't even threaten to do it ever again."

Bob actually took a moment to look as if he were thinking it over. He rubbed his chin and ran his gaze over Marcus, taking in the quality of his tailored clothes. "How do I know you'll give me the money, huh?"

"You don't have to worry about that. I'm prepared to give you a draft you can cash in any bank."

"We ain't got a bank here in Fort Regent," he whined. "I'd have to go to another town."

"Then I'll throw in travel expenses, too," Marcus said. "Is it a deal or not?"

Bob looked Angie up and down and frowned. "Yeah, it's a deal. This little wench ain't worth nothing, anyway."

"Then we'll finish our business, and you can be on your way," Marcus said crisply. He dug in his satchel and then wrote out a draft and handed it to Bob. "I'll take your copy of the agreement with the Mail Order Bride agency, too."

Bob's eyes glittered as he studied the writing. "You made yourself a lousy deal, sir, but I'm happy with my end of it. Good riddance to bad rubbish is what I say."

With that, he turned and strode out of the room, and Angie emitted a little squeal of joy. Bob Beekman was out of her life for good.

"Marcus, you are my hero, and how I love you." She wrapped her arms around him and kissed him.

"Umm, excuse me."

Angie looked up, startled, and saw Maggie and her kids standing in the entry. "Is everything … okay?"

"It is, Maggie," Marcus said. "Now, if we can just get that preacher in here, I'll marry Angie right now."

"Did I hear someone call for me?" A thick-waisted man holding a Bible walked into the room. "Are we ready to get this wedding started?"

"You bet we are," Marcus said, smiling down at Angie. "I'm more than ready to make this woman my wife."

Angie beamed up at Marcus. Tears of joy filled her eyes. She couldn't believe that just a few hours ago she'd been going to marry Bob Beekman, and now she was going to be the wife of Marcus Donahue.

She sighed happily and clung to Marcus's arm as they turned to face the preacher. Miracles really did happen.

EPILOGUE

Six Months Later

Angie opened the door of the oven and peeked inside. She was baking a birthday cake for Marcus, and she wanted it to be perfect. It was his favorite, German chocolate, and it was coming along beautifully. Just a few more minutes, and she'd pull it out.

She straightened and looked around her spacious kitchen. Every surface was spotless. She'd even already cleaned up the mixing bowl in which she'd made the cake batter.

Angie was proud of her home. It was just a couple of houses down the street from Maggie's place. She and Marcus had never returned to Boston. Instead, they had decided to stay here, and Marcus opened a much-needed bank that was doing very well for itself.

Angie still had to pinch herself. It didn't seem possible she was this happy. Even Marcus and his parents had forged a fragile truce, and they were coming for a visit next week. She was nervous about their coming, but with Marcus at her side, she knew she could face anything.

Today was Marcus's birthday, and she had written him a letter. She thought it was only appropriate since he had taught her to read and write. She didn't know of a better way to express her love and gratitude for him than to write him and try to explain her feelings.

But the letter contained more than just her gratitude. There was a surprise for him at the very end of the missive.

And you will have to wait another six months for your real present because that's how much longer it will be before our baby is born. Congratulations, Papa.

She couldn't wait to see his face when he read that part. She knew he would be delirious with joy. They had talked about having children, and Angie knew he would be a wonderful father. He was patient and kind, intelligent, and a wonderful teacher. Angie didn't know how she had gotten so lucky as to marry Marcus Donahue. It still seemed like a miracle to her.

A little later, the cake was frosted, and Marcus's supper was ready to come out of the oven when she heard his steps on the porch. Her heart skipped a beat, and she ran her hands down her apron. This was her favorite moment of the day, the moment she looked forward to every hour, every minute, that they were apart. The moment she got to kiss her husband and welcome him home.

He strode into the kitchen and gathered her close and kissed her soundly. Angie closed her eyes and enjoyed the moment. Tonight was going to be special, and her heart told her the rest of their lives was going to be special, too.

"Welcome home," she whispered in his ear.

The End

CONTINUE READING…

Thank you for reading **The Maid's Groom!** Are you wondering **what to read next?** Why not read **The Escape? Here's a peek for you:**

Garrett grabbed Betty's arm and stuck his face close to hers, spraying her with his foul breath. "Why fight me, Betty? It only makes sense. We can be married within the month."

His grip tightened, and Betty struggled to maintain her cool. She felt the pressure of his fingers through her long linen sleeve and attempted to extricate her arm. "Please, Garrett."

She worked to control her expression, hoping not to further raise his ire. His close-set black eyes bore into hers, and then he sighed and let go. She stumbled back, nearly losing her balance.

"Listen to me, Betty. My brother would have wanted this." His eyes raked over her, and she resisted the urge to flee. "You want to raise a b—?"

"Stop!" she cried. Her hand flew to her mouth. That was low even for Garrett. "My baby has two parents. He will be perfectly acceptable."

Garrett glowered, his narrow features pinched into points. "Don't forget, one of those parents is dead." He lowered his voice. "But I apologize. You're right. The baby will be accepted."

Betty's heart raced, and her breath came quickly. How could two brothers be so completely opposite? *Oh, Edmund, why did you have to die?*

She had never felt so utterly alone in her life.

Garrett laid his long bony hand on her shoulder, and she bit her lip to stifle a scream. Where could she live if he threw her out? Where could she raise her baby?

Edmund, why couldn't you have been the eldest? Why couldn't you have been the one to inherit the estate?

Garrett squeezed her shoulder brusquely, his fingers curling into her. "Mother is in complete agreement. She supports our marriage; indeed, she is pleased. After so much sadness with Edmund's passing, isn't it wise to have some celebration? Isn't it only right to give Mother joy again?"

Betty swallowed. "Edmund is hardly cold in his grave. This is no time for a marriage."

His black eyes snapped. "What is the advantage to waiting? I want this baby to belong to me. It will be a boy, and I will have an heir."

"And if it's a girl?"

"It will be a *boy*," Garrett said more strongly, obviously unwilling to acknowledge the possibility.

"You must give me more days to ponder," Betty said.

Visit HERE To Read More!

https://ticahousepublishing.com/mail-order-brides.html

MORE MAIL ORDER BRIDE ROMANCES FOR YOU!

We love clean, sweet, adventurous Mail Order Bride Romances and have a lovely library of Susannah Calloway titles just for you!

Box Sets — A Wonderful Bargain for You!

https://ticahousepublishing.com/bargains-mob-box-sets.html

Or enjoy Susannah's single titles. You're sure to find many favorites! (Remember all of them can be downloaded FREE with Kindle Unlimited!)

Sweet Mail Order Bride Romances!

https://ticahousepublishing.com/mail-order-brides.html

ABOUT THE AUTHOR

Susannah has always been intrigued with the Western movement - prairie days, mail-order brides, the gold rush, frontier life! As a writer, she's excited to combine her love of story with her love of all that is Western. Presently, Susannah lives in Wyoming with her hubby and their three amazing children.

www.ticahousepublishing.com

contact@ticahousepublishing.com

www.ingramcontent.com/pod-product-compliance
Lightning Source LLC
Chambersburg PA
CBHW051439150726
48000CB00005B/2165